This fiction book is dedicated to all of the world's racers, to the men and women who risk their lives in the name of motor sport. The grit and determination they show is outstanding and honourable, it would be a very different world without them both past and present, and this story focuses on the past and no doubt bears some resemblances to many lives in the racing world; so a big thank you to all of you, you are all champions in one way or another.

Author Derek Crysell

GW00391661

Art work by Derek Crysell

Credit to Baz & Jo Budden for the rear cover picture of Baz actually racing his Norton at the Isle of Man.

With thanks to my family Ali, Harry & Laura for putting up with me whilst I toiled away at the writing desk, love you all forever, D.

   A huge thanks to all of my friends on Normal for Norfolk Social media site for spurring me on to publish my work, you know who you are.

It was a sunny Wednesday afternoon in the village of Blakeney in Norfolk, the sky was a gorgeous blue and there was just a light breeze blowing, other than that; it was a quiet day. Tom had finished school for the day and was cycling to the paper shop to collect the papers for delivering to the villagers; on his way he passes his Grandads house. Toms Grandad was a motorbike enthusiast back in his day when he entered the Isle of Man TT race on his Norton 500 in 1954, Tom had heard all the stories over and over again told by his Grandad, of how he battled on the race track against the BSA, AJS and Triumph motorbikes in the sun wind and rain. To Tom's Grandad the Norton 500 was the bee's knees, it was sleek; it was cool, but most importantly it was flipping loud.

Tom always remembered the last story his Grandad told him; it was the time his Grandad was on his way home from the Isle of Man TT race one year and he was running late, his Grandad was meant to meeting his wife Elle for their wedding anniversary dinner at The Blakeney hotel looking out across the estuary and salt marshes, but sadly the van he was driving broke down, being an ex-military man Tom's Grandad was never ever late. The only answer was for Tom's Grandad to get the Norton 500 racing bike out of the back of the van and go for it, he put on his leather jacket, over trousers, boots and gloves , he popped his helmet on did up the strap and carefully adjusted his racing goggles.

The kick start was very difficult and hard because the compression of the engine was high since it was indeed a fully tuned racing machine, a big number four was painted on the front of the fairing, one last try of the kick start and the engine roared into life, and away he went as if he was in a race; quickly changing gear from first to second to third and fourth the Norton 500 was blasting along the road, lying flat on the tank and his head tucked behind the visor Tom's Grandad was moving like a rocket , he was doing ninety miles per hour, the trees were flying past like fence posts on a train journey, he was just coming to the brow of slight hill and he had to slow down , but a police car had just pulled out in front of him.

Tom's Grandad couldn't stop in time so he had to swerve around the two young policemen in their car, the loud noise of the Norton 500 made the policeman jump as it shot past them like a flash of lightning.

Toms Grandad kept going , he couldn't be late for his Elle, eventually he arrived at the Blakeney hotel covered in flies and bugs, he ran upstairs to find Elle sitting waiting for him, he opened the door and said "pip, pip, old girl" and gave her a huge cheeky grin, Elle was so pleased to see him.

Half an hour had passed when a police car pulled into the car park and stopped right next to the Norton 500. The two young policemen got out of their car and one of them was making notes on his notepad, and the other was looking up at the hotel, Tom's Grandad knew he was done for and just waited until the policemen came upstairs to find him. The two policemen were about the same age as Toms Grandad back then all three of them were in their thirties. Toms Grandad was eventually fined for speeding on the Queens highway; he was banned from riding his racing motorbike on public roads for good. Constable Thoroughgood attended the court case in person to make sure his man got what he deserved.

Sadly the Norton 500 was put away in his big wooden workshop at the back of his house, and there it sat for the next forty years, gathering dust.

During that time Tom's Grandad had bought an old side car to bolt onto the Norton, and he used to spend most of his time in the workshop tinkering with it, eventually Tom's Grandad became too weak to even kick start the Norton in to life, so there it sat all quiet hiding under a dusty sheet.

Tom called in to see his Grandad on his way back after he had done the paper round. "Hi Grandad" shouted Tom believing that his 15 year old voice was going to carry itself down to the bottom of the garden and through the thick workshop doors, that's where Grandad would be; with his overalls on and a spanner in his hand.

Tom wheeled his push bike down past the vegetable patch to the workshop and leant it against the workshop wall. Tom could smell hot coffee, welding smoke, and bacon sandwiches all in one sniff. There was a strange whirring noise coming from inside the workshop.

Tom opened the big wooden workshop door and saw Grandad taking a sip of coffee in one hand whilst holding his bacon sandwich in the other, "Hi Grandad" Tom said,

and Grandad turned around to face Tom with that cheeky grin he always had when he was up to something he shouldn't be. "Hi ya Tommy boy" said Grandad, "what you up to then boy?" "Well I thought I thought I better come and see you, I haven't seen you for a while, have you got a spare sandwich? I'm starving." Said Tom. "Come over here then, I made two lots so there's plenty there" "Aww thanks Grandad you're the best"

"So what have you been up to with the Norton then?" Well I don't know if I should tell you, can you keep a secret?" One side of the Norton was covered with the big dusty sheet, and Grandad was standing the other side looking rather pleased with himself; he wiped the grease from the sandwich off his chin with his sleeve and twiddled each end of his handlebar moustache to make it straight again.

"Come around this side then and have a look then Tommy boy" Tom carefully moved around the other side stepping over the spanners, welding wires and gas bottle pipes. "A sidecar" exclaimed Tom,

"Not any old sidecar Tom, I rescued this one from the Isle of Man; this sidecar was one of the first type they used." Tom Stared at it, it looked like a big bathtub with a pointy end that looked like the front end of a rocket ship, something out of the Flash Gordon comic perhaps Tom thought to himself.

"Well who's was it Grandad?" "Well back in 1954" here we go again thought Tom, "Rod Coleman from New Zealand came over to race in the TT,

" What does TT mean again Grandad?" asked Tom. "Tourist Trophy Tom, Tourist Trophy" "Anyway; as I was saying; Rod Coleman was doing a warm up round the circuit on one of the spare bikes with a sidecar attached, and he was going so fast he cut one of the corners too tight and tore it off the bike and it ended up in this young ladies garden, and that's where it sat for years wither husband growing roses in it, until I read a story in the newspaper about it, so I contacted her to see if she wanted to sell it, "Sell it?" she said "you can have it for free" she said, but I did give her a fiver for it."

"So is that all you've done, is attach a sidecar to the Norton? That's hardly a secret Grandad "Said Tom. "Not quite" said Grandad, "there's something else Tommy boy, I've only gone and fitted an electric starter instead of having to try and kick start it; did you see Grandma as you came past the house?" "No I didn't her bicycle was not tied to the carport, I bet she's gone out to the shops."

Grandad said "right let me do up this last bit then we'll give it a try, here look see this button on the handle bar? Just come and press it."

Tom pressed it and heard the whirring noise, "so that's what I could hear making that noise Grandad" "Well that is the electric motor you could hear, so when I bolt it into place it will turn the engine over and it should start, I've drained the old oil and changed the filters and put some fresh oil in and got some petrol yesterday, that old gal in the petrol station said "what do want petrol for? You hent got a car." I said it's for the lawnmower" then she said I thought you had an electric mower." "I left without saying goodbye, nosey so and so." Grandad knelt down and bolted on the starter, "there that's that on, let's gIve it a go Tommy boy.

Right, clutch is in, out of gear, engine primed, press start" a bog, bog, bog, bog, bog, bog, went the engine, "Maybe the fuels got to get through Grandad" said Tom. "Right here we go again" said Grandad, bog, bog, bog, bog ,bog, bog, bog, bog, bog, VRRRRRROOOOOOOOOOOOM VEEERRRRROOOOOOOMMMMM, The old Norton had fired up into life at last, a bit of blue smoke came out the old exhaust and drifted across the workshop. Grandad's eyes lit up like two headlights,

Tom had never seen him so happy. "Come on Tommy boy, come and have a go on the throttle" Tom leant over the sidecar to reach the throttle, a couple of quick twists on the throttle made Toms hairs on his arms stand up on end, "WOM ,WOM ,SNORT" went the engine, Tom went a bit red in the face, he thought Grandad was going to tell him off but instead Grandad stood there knowing Tom was already hooked and could appreciate the thrill of a race tuned TT Norton 500.

"Let's turn it off now Tom before we get caught, Grandma will be home soon; go and open the back door and I'll open the front one a bit to let the smell of the exhaust out." Just as Grandad was opening the front door of the workshop he saw Elle tying her bicycle to the car port and lifting a bag of groceries out of the basket from the handlebars, Grandad waved at Elle and Elle waved and smiled back, she thought to herself what he would give to ride that Motorbike one more time.

Tom and Grandad shut the doors up and started walking back up towards the house. Tom was wheeling his bicycle and Grandad was right beside him wearing a mile wide grin.

Elle looked out of the kitchen window and watched them both chatting and walking together, she knows how much Tom loved his Grandad and she knew how much she still loved him too. When they got closer to the house Grandma calls out of the window "Tom, do you want to stay for tea?" "Oh yes please Grandma." said Tom. "Ok I'll phone your mum and tell her you won't be home just yet, you know how your mum worries about you."

"You two can wash your hands before you sit at my table." Said Elle; with slight smile, Tom and Grandad playfully pushing each other as they both tried to wash their hands at the same sink. "Whoops" said Grandad as the bar of soap shot out of his hands and got tangled up in the net curtain nearly breaking the china duck that sat on the tiled window ledge; his cousin had bought it as a wedding present for them all those years ago.

"Sausage beans and mash ok for you Tom?" "Thanks Grandma; that's just perfect." All three of them sat; eating chatting and Grandad thinking about his Norton 500; "WOM,WOM, SNORT"

Tom helped to wash up, Grandad dried the dishes and Grandma put them away in their special places in her neat cupboards. "It'll soon be getting dark Tom have you got lights on your bicycle?" said Grandad.

"Yes all ship shape Captain," Said Tom raising his hand in a salute and grinning from ear to ear.

Grandad and Elle stood in the kitchen doorway to wave Tom off, "Hurry up before it gets too dark" Shouted Grandad. "Ok "said Tom. Just as Tom reached the road; a bright red Ferrari drove past very slowly, it was a thirty mile per hour speed limit, but it was only doing about twenty, the driver was wearing dark sunglasses and a blue sports jacket with two white stripes down the sleeve. Tom turned to look at his Grandad and pulled a face to indicate "That was a posh car"

Tom waved goodbye to them both and then got on the road to cycle home, in the distance Tom could just about see the tail lights of the Ferrari, unmistakable big round back lights.

"Have you finished polishing that suit of armour for the village fete for this Saturday?" Said Elle, "Yes nearly finished it, I'm not sure that it still fits me though said Grandad."

It was the local village fete at the weekend and Grandad was supposed to be part of a reconstruction of the Knights of the Round Table, but unbeknown to him Elle had been in contact with his old racing buddies and they were all going to turn up dressed as knights and surprise him.

The weekend of the village fete was one day away, Ring, ring, ring, ring. "Hello Tom speaking" "Hi Tom its Grandma, can you talk?" "Of course I can, I have all the time in the world for you Grandma" said Tom, "Well Tom; I have a favour to ask of you", "Yes sure anything for you" said Tom.

Elle went on to explain to Tom that this Saturday was the village fete and that Grandad was taking part in a reconstruction of the knights of the Round Table, and that he would be wearing a suit of armour, and that she had invited all of his old racing buddies along and that they would be wearing suits of armour too , but the best and tricky bit is that they are all bringing their Racing motor bikes along and that somehow and Tom's Dad was to try and Grandads Norton 500 to the fete without him knowing, Tom was really excited at the thought of it all.

Elle went on to explain the plan of how they were going to do it, the plan was; that on the morning of the fete Tom would ring up and ask Grandad to come and help him mend a puncture on his bicycle and help him sort his brakes out, in the meantime Toms Dad and a friend would get the get the Norton & sidecar onto a trailer and get it to the fete whilst he was helping Tom. Grandad would be running short of time and there was no way he would even go in to his workshop on that morning as he would know that he had to get changed in to his suit of armour "That's a great idea grandma." said Tom.

"Ok let me speak to your dad then please." said Elle. After the phone call had finished everybody had agreed on the plan and knew exactly what they had to do.

Saturday morning had arrived. Beep, beep, beep, beep. "Oh turn that alarm off Elle please is it 7:30 already? Do you want a cup of tea and a slice of buttered toast?" "Oh yes please, but don't you have too many slices or you won't get that suit of armour on today." said Elle laughing into her pillow.

Dead on half past eight Grandads phone rings, "Hello" "Hi Grandad it's Tom, sorry to bother you but do you think you could help me this morning with my bicycle, I have a puncture and my brakes need adjusting too?" "Oh Tom what a day to ask, I got to get ready for the fete; I have to be there at ten this morning." "Oh Please Grandad, Mum and Dad are helping out at the fete and they are leaving early and I need my bicycle so I can get there on time myself, pleeeeeaase." "Oh ok then, it better not take too long though, I hate being late." "Thanks Grandad you're the best." Grandad told Elle what the telephone call had been about, Elle Said "He knows how to pick a strange time doesn't he".

"Well I can't let him down he's a good kid." said Grandad.

Grandad arrived at Tom's house to find Tom with his wheel and tyre off, sitting on the lawn with his inner tube in a bowl of water watching the bubbles. "Hi ya Tommy boy got some trouble have we?" "Well I'm not sure Grandad it seems to be coming from the valve." "Has your dad got a toolkit in his garage Tom?" "I think so; I'll go and have a look." Tom emerged from the garage carrying a small toolkit roll, they undid it and found a small tool to tighten the valve up, they pumped some air back in it and stuck the valve under the water again, no bubbles this time. "Well done Grandad I knew you could fix it."

"Now what's up with those brakes my boy?"

Well they do work but I have to pull the lever all the way back before anything happens." "Ah that'll because the brake blocks have worn down, I'll just readjust them and they should be fine." Just as Grandad had finished adjusting Tom's brakes they both heard a low rumbling noise coming down the road, then they saw what it was, the big red Ferrari slowly drove by with the same man driving it from the previous night, "He's driving that slow Grandad, don't you think.?

"The trouble is Tommy boy, some of these people like to think they're flash but haven't got two pennies to rub together, and you'll soon learn that in life son, he probably can't afford the petrol." "Anyway that's all fixed, what's the time Tommy lad?" "It's twenty past nine Grandad fancy a cuppa?" "Twenty past flipping nine" Shouted Grandad, "I've got to get going, I'm going to be late, I've got to get that blooming suit of armour on yet." "I'll phone dad and get him to pick you up in the van in half an hour." "Thanks Tommy boy" said Grandad.

At twenty minutes to ten, Tom's dad pulls up outside Grandad's house in his van only to find Elle trying to push a big pointy helmet on Grandad's head, "come on bring it with you we'll put it on when we get there." shouted Toms Dad. Grandad, Elle and the pointy Helmet were on the front seat of the van in under a minute. "I see you got the suit on ok, it looks really authentic." said Tom's Dad. "Authentic?" "It's a real suit of armour you cheeky devil, I paid a fortune for this years ago." "Was that when you were fighting for King Arthur? ha, ha, ha." Tom's dad laughed, and Grandad twiddled his moustache.

When they arrived at the fete there were tables and stalls receiving their final touches before the grand opening, there were cake stalls, tombola's, a giant marrow completion table, darts game, skittles, even the three village Police motor bikes and one police car were there too; ready for the onslaught of children to have their photos taken by their parents whilst sitting on the bikes or in the car; but the centre piece was the big round table that was placed in front of cardboard castle that had been painted by the local school arts teacher and pupils.

"Right let's get this helmet on you" said Elle. Grandad managed to sit on the step of the van whilst Elle and Tom's Dad wriggled it onto his head, "There, it's on" Said Tom's Dad; "and be careful when you turn around; you could have someone's eye out with that pointy nose cone" at that point Tom arrived just in time on his bicycle.

They all led Grandad to the round table, the table actually only had enough seats for six knights but as we know as legend has it; King Arthur had many more knights.

As soon as Grandad was seated two Trumpeters walked from each side of the castle and began to play a tune loosely sounding like the Purcell trumpet tune from the film of King Arthur; there were a couple of high notes that shouldn't have been where they were but it didn't sound too bad.

The villagers had all assembled to see the grand opening, the Town Mayor had arrived along with the Town Crier and his big brass bell; as the trumpeters were doing their best; five other knights walked from behind the castle and took their places around the table, all of the suits of armour were gleaming and their pointy nose cones were all facing each other after being seated. The trumpeters fell silent. The Town Crier raised his bell and rang it loudly three times; then he cried out "OH YEY, OH YEY, OH YEY, ON THIS DAY WE CELEBRATE TOGETHER OUR ANNUAL VILLAGE FETE; LET THERE BE FUN AND MUCH MERRIMENT; OH YEY, OH YEY, OH YEY" everyone clapped and cheered, the Town Mayor then cut the red ribbon to the entrance of the fete and everyone cheered again.

The Mayor led the villagers into the fete arena and stopped short of the round table where the six Knights were seated perfectly still and looking as if they were statues; whilst all this was going on there was an unfamiliar face in the crowd, he was looking sneaky, and was wondering about pretending to look at the police motorbikes and car, he then bought a single cream bun from one of the stalls and then walked away from the fete. The Mayor said to everyone "we can all feel safe here today because we are being protected by the Knights of the Round Table; they will be performing their swordsmanship skills to us later on this morning, but before we do anything else we must see who our fine Knights are."

The Mayor pointed at Grandad and said "Kind Sir please raise your helmet and reveal your identity" Grandad raised his helmet being very careful not to bend his handlebar moustache, and smiled and nodded graciously at the crowd's applause. The Mayor then said "Please can all the other Knights raise their helmets to reveal your identities".

The other five Knights raised their helmets at the same time and Grandad immediately recognised them all, they were his Isle of Man T.T racing buddies, Grandad could not believe his eyes; then he shouted out their names one by one; "Alistair, Danny, Dave, Eric and Percy" Elle had tears of joy running down her face, she knew she had made him the happiest man on the planet, Elle hugged Tom and thanked him for his help.

The Mayor bellowed "We must see our shining Knights steeds, remove the castle wall", everyone expected to see six horses but were surprised to see six vintage racing motorbikes stood side by side, there were two Triumphs, a BSA, an Arial and two Norton 500's, Grandad saw his beloved Norton with the unmistakable number four painted on the fairing; his hairs on his neck stood up on end, all the other machines also had sidecars fitted too , Grandad said "I can't believe you all have sidecars" Eric shouted out "Well it's better than having stabilisers at our age" and they all laughed together just like they used to years ago.

The villagers were busy playing games and buying things from the stalls, there were as predicted children queuing up to have their photos taken next the police car and motorbikes. Suddenly the lady who runs the petrol station came racing up in her car and did a huge skid in the dust at the side of the road, she jumped out of her car and ran straight to the Policemen who were talking to the Town Crier, "what's wrong" said one of the policemen, the petrol station lady blurted out "there's been a robbery at the post office and at the Manor house, and all the phone lines have been cut, the butler of the Manor house saw a red sports car driving away at speed"

"Did he get a good look at the person" said the policeman? "Yes he was wearing a blue top with white stripes on the sleeves and he had sun glasses on." Tom was standing close by and heard everything, "Excuse me Sir" said Tom to the policeman, "but Grandad, Grandma and I saw a red sports car driving around slowly twice this week and that description fits the driver, and the car is a Ferrari; a red Ferrari."

The Town Crier starts to ring his bell, "OH NO, OH NO, THERE'S BEEN A ROBBERY AT THE POST OFFICE AND AT THE MANOR HOUSE AND THE MAYORS WIFES JEWELLERY HAS BEEN STOLEN, OH NO, OH NO"

The policemen run to their bikes and car, they are trying to radio the police station to get details. The crowd starts talking, one of the policemen shouts "the phone lines are not the only things that have been cut, our break lines and radio wires have been cut too; he must have been here this morning when we were setting everything up" "ooooh, the cheek of him" said the cake stall lady, "he bought one of my cream buns, he lifted the glass lid off without asking." Tom butted in, "was he wearing gloves?" "No he wasn't, I know that because he had nasty hairy hands." "Brilliant then we should have his finger prints" said Tom, "Good thinking lad" said the policeman.

"Which way was the car travelling from the Manor young lady?" the butler said it turned left heading towards Sheringham" the policeman smiled and said "Well he won't be going far then because all the roads have been blocked off for the workmen and the new drainage systems that are going in today,

I know he's got to turn round and he will be heading back this way." "But how are we going to catch him Sergeant? Our brakes are no good and we don't have radios." said one of the young policemen. Just then a shiny nose cone nearly poked the sergeant in the ear, "if you need transport we've got just what you need, it was one of the famous racing heroes offering their racing machines and sidecars for service

"Quick to the bikes" shouted the Sergeant, "hang on, hang on," said Grandad, "you can't ride these on the road they're not street legal, I got fined and banned years ago for that," The Sergeant looked at the bike and went almost white with fear, it can't be can it? "can't be what" said Grandad, The police Sergeant found it hard to say; but eventually managed to spit it out in a wobbly voice, "is that the Norton 500 , number 4 from 1954?" Grandad said "Why yes it is, why?" because I am or was constable Thoroughgood; and I know how fast that can thing can go.

Just at that point the high tone and tuned engine noise of a speeding car could be heard in the distance changing gears for the bends in the road, it sounded like it was really moving fast.

Grandad shouted "To the bikes lads get them started up." The six Knights in shining armour ran to their bikes, the three motorbike policemen followed them and jumped into a side car each, Grandad got to his Norton 500 turned the ignition on and hit the new starter button, Bog, bog, bog, bog, bog, boom, WOM, WOM, WOM went the engine,

Sargent Thoroughgood stood back as Tom ran past him nearly knocking him over and gingerly jumping into Grandads sidecar, the other police car driver got in another sidecar, and the lady from the cake stall jumped into the last sidecar shouting "I'm not going to miss this for the world." As they started making their way to the exit; the Town Mayor was shouting "May god be with you all."

The lady from the petrol station was handing out two wooden skittles to the sidecar passengers; the cake lady said "what do I want them for." "Throwing my dear, these are for throwing at that rotten burglar." And the petrol station lady jumped in to the last side car as it was coming past her.

Just then the red Ferrari shot past the entrance to the fete at high speed.

"That's him lets go" shouted one of the police men, Grandad looked down at Tom and winked, he said "do you remember all the stories I told you about cornering with sidecars and how you have to lean with the corners?" "Yes Grandad of course I do." said Tom, Elle stood at the exit, she took her bright blue scarf off and quickly tied it round Grandads right arm, he truly was her Knight in shining armour "Good luck my love, and look after Tom for goodness sake" said Elle.

"Of course I will, toodle pip old girl; I'll see you later for tea when we get back" said grandad. Grandad closed the nose cone on his suit of armour and he slipped the Norton into first gear, he got off the grass and on to the tarmac road, he straightened it up and said to Tom "Hang on Tommy Boy let's show them what we've got." WOM , WOM ,

Grandad let go of the clutch he wound the throttle back the rev counter blipped round to the red band in a split second, 2nd gear engine revs speed increasing 3rd and then forth gear and they were out of sight, the rest of the pack was behind him, what a sight to see, six knights in shining armour three policemen, Tom, and the cake stall lady holding her hat on and holding two skittles under her other arm and the nosey woman from the petrol station.

They were already gaining on the Ferrari as it kept having to slow down for the bends but the bikes were almost at full throttle on each turn, the motorbike policemen were loving every second of it, especially leaning out of the sidecar to keep the weight even with the bike as they went into the corners hard.

Meanwhile back at the fete amongst all the excitement and confusion Toms Dad said to Elle "Where's Tom?" Elle said "He's gone with Grandad" "You are kidding me?" said Tom's Dad, "get in the van were going to help them." Sargent Thoroughgood said "well if you have room I would like to come along too." All three of them got in the van and chased after the pack.

Three miles up the road the chase was heating up, as Tom and Grandad blasted around one of the bends they just caught a glimpse of the back end of the Ferrari as is disappeared around the corner head, The burglar had no idea that he had six professional TT Racers on his tail armed with three policemen, Tom, the Cake lady and ten wooden skittles, and a nosey woman.

With the next bend out of the way all the bikes could open up full throttle on the straight, The bikes were riding five abreast across the road, dust was flying up behind

them, they looked like a steel tank whizzing down the road;

Grandad zoomed right up behind the Ferrari, he was actually rubbing his front tyre on the rear bumper, "Right Tom; chuck a skittle through his back window" "Yes Sir" shouted Tom. Tom threw a wooden skittle right through the back window of the Ferrari; "Smash".

The burglar swerved almost uncontrollably as it made him jump, he looked in his rear view mirror and could not believe what he was seeing, a man wearing a suit of armour riding a motorbike right on his tail. Suddenly the burglar braked hard and Grandad had to swerve but the sidecar hit the back of the car with so much force it bent the chassis, and the sidecar was not running straight at all, Grandad eased off the accelerator and said to Tom "sorry Tommy boy I've got to ditch the side car" he slowed right down, and kicked a release lever that he had installed and the sidecar detached from the Norton; by this time the Ferrari had got ahead by some distance, the rest of the pack caught them up just as Tom had come to a standstill , Grandad said "Catch ya later Alligator" and shot off like a rocket after the burglar again.

The main pack was about 15 seconds behind him, but unbeknown to Grandad the burglar had turned the Ferrari around and was heading straight back towards Grandad, 98.99.100 miles per hour, the Norton 500 was flying , the suspension was behaving on each bump of the road, a nice smooth fast ride, a brow of a hill was coming up, Grandad let go of the throttle a bit, but total horror, it was stuck wide open, in a split second he and the Ferrari met square on at the brow of the hill, it was all in slow motion, The pack behind Grandad saw it all as he ploughed right into the front of it, Grandad was thrown from the Norton and out of site over the top of a hedge, the Ferrari was hit so badly it lost control and smashed into the ditch at the side of the road spraying mud and bits of car everywhere; all the other bikes and sidecars came to a screeching halt with smoke billowing off their tyres.

Toms Dad had picked Tom up from the sidecar on their way past.

when they arrived they saw the dreadful mess. A piece of the Norton 500 fairing was laying on the grass verge with its number four facing towards heaven, all the TT Racers had surrounded the robber in the smashed Ferrari, with the police. Elle got out of the van with Sergeant Thoroughgood and Toms Dad. Elle couldn't understand why there were only five Knights in shining armour.

Then she saw the famous number four lying helpless on the grass verge and close by was her bright blue scarf she had tied to his arm, Elle loved that man so much, they had spent all their life together, she broke down in floods of tears, Sergeant Thoroughgood put his arm around her to try and comfort her, Tom sat on the verge staring at the number four with tears rolling down his cheeks.

All the noise had stopped, the Norfolk wind blew gently across the fields, and everyone took a moment of silence and bowed their heads.

All of a sudden from the other side of the hedge someone shouted "will someone come and get me out of this blooming suit of armour" Grandad was alive, he had actually landed head first into a haystack, they all ran through a gap in the hedge to find him sitting upright and his nose cone was bent at a right angle, when he saw Elle he shouted "Pip, Pip; old girl, did I get him? I told you I'd see you later for tea."

Sergeant Thoroughgood approached him smiling; he said "you really remind me of somebody from years ago, he was a racer with a Norton 500!!

Now what's your name Sir?" "My Name?" said Grandad. "My name is Rod Coleman from New Zealand." Tom fell over backwards with surprise, not only was his Grandad alive but his Grandad was the winner and real champion of the Isle Of Man TT race in 1954. Tom and Elle hugged him; Tom said why did you change your name?" Grandad said "he couldn't have lived with the shame of being banned under his real name and he didn't want to bring a dark cloud over his mates and all the other TT racers."

Sergeant Thoroughgood said; "I'm so sorry Rod, I was only doing my job." Grandad said "Well I was only doing ninety; well at least we can say we got all the lolly back from the burglar". "So Tommy boy, next project, rebuilding a Norton 500, not just any old Norton 500 , THE Norton 500, Did I ever tell you the story about". Here we go again thought Tom, but his Grandad really was the best.

To be continued……………………………..

Printed in Great Britain
by Amazon